She Is Myth

Ancel Mondia

Ukiyoto Publishing

All global publishing rights are held by

Ukiyoto Publishing

Published in 2024

Content Copyright © Ancel Mondia
ISBN 9789362691958

*All rights reserved.
No part of this publication may be reproduced,
transmitted, or stored in a retrieval system, in any form
by any means, electronic, mechanical, photocopying,
recording or otherwise, without the prior permission of
the publisher.*

The moral rights of the authors have been asserted.

*This is a work of fiction. Names, characters, businesses,
places, events, locales, and incidents are either the
products of the author's imagination or used in a fictitious
manner. Any resemblance to actual persons, living or
dead, or actual events is purely coincidental.*

*This book is sold subject to the condition that it shall not by
way of trade or otherwise, be lent, resold, hired out or
otherwise circulated, without the publisher's prior
consent, in any form of binding or cover other than that in
which it is published.*

www.ukiyoto.com

Contents

Phoenix	1
Unicorn	6
Undine	11
Dragon	15
Werewolf	19
Sylph	23
About the Author	*27*

Phoenix

In a typical village where ordinary men and women were orderly clustered around a central point which was suitably occupied by a simple church, feebly came the aged head villager, shakingly carrying his only one yet severely ill child.

The sobbing head villager slowly placed his dying daughter on the vacant altar, submissively knelt and emotionally prayed for the healing grace from the invisible entity that seemed to quietly exist in front of him.

He was humbly uttering his personal prayers when all of a sudden, his rushing aged wife appeared right behind him.

"My dear husband, weep no more. We still have hope." His wife spoke with pure delight.

The melancholic eyes of the head villager abruptly lighted up, as he swiftly turned to exactly face his hurrying wife.

"Where are you going, my wife?" He asked in pleasant surprise.

"I'll be welcoming the sage healer. Oh, here she comes!" His wife exclaimed with anticipation as she joyfully stood at the opened door.

The head villager rapidly followed his hopeful wife, and calmly yet bravely walking towards them was a woman clothed in warm and bright fabrics.

The teary eyes of the aged couple gradually widened as the vibrant woman slowly came near to them.

When the vibrant woman steadily stood before the aged couple, she powerfully asked. "Where is your daughter?"

Upon obviously hearing the clear question of the vibrant woman, the aged couple swiftly moved to the sides of the door to freely open the narrow way towards the altar where their dying daughter was silently lying down.

The vibrant woman instantly fixed her mysterious eyes on the severely ill child. She simply passed by the aged couple and quietly walked towards the altar. The aged couple immediately followed the vibrant woman.

The vibrant woman clearly spoke. "I am Phoenix, the sage healer."

The aged couple suddenly rejoiced in gratitude for the expected healing of their only child.

Phoenix gradually knelt before the dying child, as the rest of the villagers curiously gathered inside the church to witness her miracle of healing.

Phoenix gently touched the thin and pale arm of the severely ill child. The aged couple closely observed their dying daughter.

The child was slowly and weakly breathing, and all of a sudden, her breathing completely stopped.

The light in the eyes of the head villager abruptly died upon closely witnessing the physical death of his only child under the hand of the sage healer.

His aged wife crazily cried and tightly embraced their lifeless daughter, as the rest of the villagers totally turned silent in shock and disbelief.

Phoenix instantly and terrifyingly released the dead child. With shame in her dimmed face, she confusedly looked around her.

The pained head villager suddenly turned wildly mad and strongly pointed a trembling finger to the sage healer.

"You are a killer! You killed my daughter!" He spoke with anger and hurt.

Phoenix frighteningly shook her head and emotionally cried to helplessly defend herself. "No! I'm not a killer! I am the sage healer! I don't know. I don't know what happened. But I didn't kill her. I don't kill!"

All of a sudden, the villagers around the sage healer wildly threw countless stones at her. Phoenix confusedly screamed in pain, and when she was obviously about to run, she was abruptly captured by the villagers.

Phoenix was violently dragged outside the church, and smelly oil was abruptly poured on her. She was forcefully pushed on the dusty ground, and a fiery torch was thrown at her.

The deadly fire shockingly crawled around her oiled body, as she horribly cried in fatal pain.

All of a sudden, she turned silent and motionless.

The merciless fire gradually extinguished, and expectedly left on the ground were typical ashes.

The enraged head villager, weakly carrying his lifeless child, quietly followed by his mourning wife and the sympathizing villagers, painfully condemned the ashes of the sage healer.

Suddenly, from the ashes grew fires that felt warm and looked bright, and shockingly gathered as one to clearly form a standing flaming figure of a huge bird.

The fiery bird spread her vibrant wings and opened her fierce eyes, clear tears gradually dropped down her feathered face.

Phoenix instantly readied herself to freely fly, and when her two feet highly lifted from the dusty ground, she forcibly turned her back as her remaining ashes scattered in the invisible air.

The ashes of the resurrected sage healer slowly fell on the pale skin of the lifeless child, and all of a sudden, the dead daughter breathed again.

The entire villagers were utterly surprised, and in guilt and shame, they stared at Phoenix flying away towards the horizon surrounded with warmth and light.

Unicorn

At the pine-forested mountain with cold weather and foggy surroundings, two distinguished tribes solemnly gathered to closely witness the wedding ceremony of the male chief of the one tribe, and the daughter of the female chief of the other tribe.

The female chief and her uniformed tribe orderly grouped themselves at one side, and the other ruly tribe steadily stayed at the side where the male chief mightily stood as the proud groom in the wedding ceremony.

The grassy narrow aisle obviously separated the two distinguished tribes, and as the skilled musicians wonderfully played their native instruments, the youthful bride in plain white dress expectedly showed up to smoothly walk down the aisle.

The female chief silently stared at her straight-faced daughter slowly proceeding towards the proud groom and the nondescript minister.

When the youthful bride and the proud groom quietly faced the nondescript minister, the two distinguished tribes solemnly watched the wedding ceremony.

"Chief, do you take Unicorn to be your wedded wife, to live together in marriage?" The minister clearly asked.

With pride in his face and voice, the male chief replied. "I do."

"Unicorn, do you take Chief to be your wedded husband, to live together in marriage?" The minister expectedly asked Unicorn.

Unicorn was straight-faced and tight-lipped.

Her silent mother was obviously shocked, and her uniformed tribe randomly looked confused.

The nondescript minister audibly repeated the clear question.

Unicorn's eyes visibly turned wet, and tears suddenly fell down her youthful face. She slowly shook her adorned head, and forcibly answered with a trembling voice. "No!"

The two distinguished tribes all together gasped in shock and disbelief.

The female chief abruptly turned red in anger and shame, as she mightily yelled at the emotional bride.

"What are you doing, Unicorn?! You're putting us in shame!"

The proud groom obviously lost his masculine composure, as he madly whispered to Unicorn.

"What a disgrace you are. What a scene you've made."

Upon closely witnessing the unfavorable reaction of her enraged mother and disconcerted groom, Unicorn gradually gained the audacity to speak in resentment.

"No! I will not marry this man! I will not obey that woman! I have enough! I will not offer my body and share my soul with somebody I don't love. I will not go against the meaning of marriage."

The female chief madly argued. "You don't know what you're saying, Unicorn! Marry Chief! For the union and survival of our tribes! Look at them. They all depend on you."

Unicorn's youthful face was extremely contorted in pain and indignation, as she emotionally answered.

"I am pure. Marriage is supposed to be pure. I will not sacrifice my purity for your sake! I am a woman of worth! I don't deserve this!"

Unicorn suddenly walked out from her wedding ceremony, and ran straight towards the thick fog.

Her mighty groom extremely trembled in madness and shame, and he swiftly grabbed a long and sharp spear.

Unicorn expectedly went through the thick fog, and a deadly spear speedily followed her.

Behind the thick fog shockingly came an ear-splitting scream that extremely disturbed the senses of the two distinguished tribes.

The female chief crazily cried as she unexpectedly witnessed the sudden death of her youthful daughter and the unseen betrayal of the male chief.

"Unicorn!"

Her uniformed tribe furiously attacked the other tribe that was swift to skillfully defend their male chief.

All of a sudden, disturbing waving of feathered wings, instantly followed by weighty footsteps seemingly paralyzed the two distinguished tribes.

The thick fog gradually thinned and disappeared, and before the two distinguished tribes stood a white horse with one sharp horn and feathered wings.

The two distinguished tribes were in extreme confusion and fear, and the female chief loudly begged for forgiveness.

"Unicorn, my daughter. I'm begging you. Please, forgive me."

The white horse simply nodded as an obvious response, and she graciously spread her feathered wings to skillfully fly towards the thick white clouds above the pine-forested mountain.

Unicorn wondrously flew away as she certainly carried with her the purity of her soul.

Undine

On a fair summer day, when the gentle wind typically formed spilling waves on the calm surface of the open water, a young lady with flowing long hair, with two teen girls behind her, leisurely walked on the white sandy seashore.

They delightedly observed the behaved sea and the good weather, and their feminine faces gradually showed a sense of safety.

The young lady slowly approached the spilling waves as she gladly stepped in the open water.

She surprisingly turned around to obviously face the two teen girls, and she brightly smiled and excitedly talked to them.

"Sisters, join me! The water feels safe and rewarding."

The two teen girls widely smiled as a response, they happily exchanged stares, willingly nodded, and quickly joined the young lady in the open water.

The youthful sisters obviously savored the behaved sea and the good weather, as their skins beautifully turned wet and bright.

A teen girl excitedly spoke. "Sister Undine, please train us to swim better."

Another teen girl instantly agreed. "Yes, Sister Undine. We want to learn more from you."

Undine sweetly smiled in front of her two teen sisters.

A teen girl proudly continued. "I like how you teach swimming. Your instructions are clear, just like this water."

Another teen girl immediately nodded. "Yes, and you swim so beautifully like these waves."

Undine grinned widely, and gladly replied to her two teen sisters. "Thank you for your compliments, sisters."

She willingly nodded, and audibly spoke. "Yes, I'll teach you how to swim."

The two teen girls instantly exclaimed in happiness and excitement.

The youthful sisters happily spent the fair summer day swimming in the open water.

Undine was deeply focused on one of her teen sisters, when all of a sudden, her sweet smile obviously faded.

She instantly looked panicked, and when she quickly looked over her shoulder, her eyes extremely widened in fear.

Her other teen sister was desperately trying to save herself from the obvious danger of drowning.

Undine quickly swam to hopefully rescue her drowning sister that was meters away from her.

She speedily reached her drowning sister, and mightily lifted her from the open water.

Undine obviously was about to effortlessly carry her teen sister, when extreme shock abruptly was shown in her young face.

She hesitantly released her teen sister, and confusingly spoke.

"Go now. Swim back to the shore."

Her teen sister doubtfully responded. "What about you?!"

Undine instantly began to have a tough expression in her wet and bright face, as she mightily spoke.

"Go now! Save yourselves!"

Her teen sister was obviously shocked, yet she confusingly obeyed her.

The two teen girls quickly swam back to the white sandy seashore, and when they frighteningly turned around, they emotionally witnessed Undine that was painfully drowning.

"Sister Undine!"

Undine unexpectedly got drowned in the open water that had calm surface, and spilling waves that were typically formed by the gentle wind.

The teary eyes of the two teen girls steadily stared at the behaved sea.

All of a sudden, from the exact area where Undine completely submerged, transparent water gradually emerged.

The two teen girls shockingly realized that the transparent water was an obvious figure of Undine.

She seemingly turned into a fluid creature with mirror-like eyes that had a look of safety.

Undine slowly and simply submerged in the open water, on a fair summer day.

Dragon

Before the large entrance of the hollow space of the cave landform in the verdant mountain, conceitedly stood a middle-aged woman who obviously acted as the aloof owner of the rock formation.

The middle-aged woman seemingly lived all alone in the verdant mountain, and firmly treated the cave landform as her very own home.

She even strongly carried some wood logs, and skillfully built a controllable bonfire at the vacant opening of the cave landform.

The middle-aged woman apparently had a natural frown that permanently made her look as an ill-tempered and threatening inhabitant of the verdant mountain.

She conceitedly walked around the cave landform like a bold guardian that diligently acted on her noble duty.

All of a sudden, the aloof owner of the rock formation clearly heard the repeated crunching sound of dried leaves.

The controllable bonfire gradually extinguished, and the bright day instantly spread its warm light in the verdant mountain.

The conceited woman boldly stood in front of the large entrance of the cave landform, as she obviously expected the literal appearance of the unknown beings that repeatedly caused the crunching sound.

She gradually began to look more ill-tempered and threatening as her natural frown became more prominent in her middle-aged face.

Before her anticipatedly appeared the two foreign men who were obviously surprised upon suddenly seeing her conceited face.

The two foreign men instantly looked threatened, and inaudibly whispered to each other.

They hesitantly proceeded towards the conceited woman, and nervously smiled.

"Hello." The two foreign men confusingly greeted her.

With masculine and furious voice, the conceited woman spoke. "Get out of my place!"

The two foreign men were instantly shocked, but quickly regained their manly composure.

One of them bravely spoke. "Woman, what is behind you?"

The conceited woman frowned more. "I am Dragon, and it's my home."

The other foreign man calmly talked to her. "Woman, tell us. Are there crystals inside your home?"

Dragon suddenly looked alarmed, as she quickly pulled out a sharp dagger and pointed at the two foreign men.

"Stay away from my home!" She bravely said.

The two foreign men wickedly smiled, and shockingly pulled out metal guns and pointed at Dragon.

The aloof owner of the rock formation naively looked at the metal guns, and in unison the two foreign men pulled the trigger.

Dragon was fatally shot in the head and heart, but instead of falling dead, her opened eyes suddenly blazed and the scorching fire swiftly crawled all over her standing body.

All of a sudden, the deadly fire was seemingly blown away, and instead of a standing woman, the two foreign men shockingly saw a large lizard with wide wings and a barbed tail.

The two foreign men abruptly looked extremely threatened, and when they obviously were about to run, the conceited creature heavily breathed and strongly blew fire at them.

When the scorching fire gradually ceased burning, the two foreign men physically turned into lifeless ashes.

Dragon nonchalantly turned her back, and simply entered the cave landform, and slowly disappeared in its contained darkness.

Werewolf

In the middle of the cold night, when the full moon brightly shone upon the dense forest where a small shack was weakly built, an untidy woman was gently carrying a toddler boy in her motherly arms.

The untidy woman was physically thin and pale, and had several bruises on her rough skin, while the toddler boy plainly looked unwell and unhealthy.

When the toddler boy was about to drowsily shut his sad eyes, the creaking door suddenly opened, and the untidy woman obviously panicked.

A drunk man slowly entered the small shack, and fiercely stared at the untidy woman who gently placed her shocked son in the toddler bed.

The drunk man quickly walked towards the untidy woman, and strongly slapped her rough face.

The untidy woman looked extremely hurt, and with teary eyes and trembling lips, she asked.

"What did I do wrong?"

The drunk man visibly looked furious and forcefully shouted at the untidy woman.

"Shame on you! Look at yourself! You're so disgusting! Filthy and stinking! I don't deserve you as my wife."

The untidy woman abruptly turned tight-lipped.

The drunk man quickly looked at the obviously afraid toddler, mightily carried him, and angrily spoke to the silenced woman.

"I am breaking up with you! I am bringing my son with me!"

The filthy and stinking woman suddenly looked startled, and emotionally spoke.

"No! Don't take our son away from me. I am his mother."

She weakly tried to physically grab the toddler boy from the muscular arms of the drunk man, but his weighty fist strongly hit her.

She was violently pushed by the cruel hand of the drunk man, but she relentlessly tried to get the toddler boy back in her motherly arms.

All of a sudden, she strongly bit the muscular arms of the drunk man, and he loudly screamed in great pain.

He mindlessly released the toddler boy, but when the untidy woman was about to physically reach for the confused toddler, the drunk man suddenly grabbed her thin neck.

The drunk man threateningly spoke. "Where are you going, Werewolf?"

The choking woman painfully stuttered. "Leave my son alone. If I can't protect him, you can't harm him, either."

The drunk man forcefully shouted at her. "Enough!"

He quickly slapped her rough face, and the toddler boy suddenly cried.

"Mama!"

The filthy and stinking woman bravely faced her crying son.

"Run, my son! I can no longer protect you. From now on, please protect yourself. Free yourself from hurt. Please, live a life. Run!"

A weighty fist violently hit her, and the toddler boy confusingly exited through the opened door.

As the drunk man repeatedly hit her, the untidy woman was about to weakly shut her teary eyes, when suddenly, the violent man hurtfully pulled his weighty fist back.

The teary eyes of the filthy and stinking woman were extremely bulged, and her shut lips shockingly elongated.

Dark and thick hair rapidly grew all over her feminine body, as she gradually stood straight before the violent man.

He closely beheld the actual appearance of the horrible beast right in front of him.

"Werewolf?" He uttered in great cowardice.

All of a sudden, Werewolf mightily lifted her sharp and long claws, and horribly sliced the violent man.

She nonchalantly went outside the small shack, and calmly stared at the toddler boy confusingly running away through the dense forest lighted up by the full moon.

Werewolf gradually turned her back, quietly proceeded in a different direction, and resoundingly howled in the middle of the cold night.

Sylph

At the center of the broad and flat land where countless grasses freely grew, a bamboo house was humbly built and quietly occupied by a slender and fair lady.

Her gentle presence was seemingly unnoticed by other live beings, but her physical existence certainly occupied a good spot in the vast plain.

The slender and fair lady was like the vast plain that wonderfully had a peaceful atmosphere and a beautiful appearance.

Both the gentle lady and the grassy plain silently existed and harmoniously connected to each other as they were untouched and undisturbed by external forces.

All of a sudden, the gentle lady was awakened by the loud sound of the approaching huge trucks.

She confusingly opened her bamboo door and surprisingly saw several trucks slowly stopped nearby in the vast plain.

She instantly looked alarmed when several men randomly went out of the huge trucks, and deliberately took out brick and concrete blocks.

The unknown men actively placed the heavy blocks on the grassy ground, and the gentle lady obviously looked offended as she quietly observed them.

She abruptly heard the unknown men mockingly laughing as they effortfully continued their disturbing activity.

The slender and fair lady hardly controlled her obvious anger, and rapidly went to the unknown men as she loudly shooed them away.

"Stop! Stop what you're doing! Leave this place! Go away!"

The unknown men were confusingly interrupted from their disturbing activity, and surprisingly looked at the gentle lady.

"What are you saying, lady?" One of the unknown men teasingly asked.

The slender and fair lady bravely stood before the unknown men and clearly spoke.

"I am Sylph. I am telling you to stop putting your blocks here. Bring them back with you and leave this place."

The unknown men mockingly laughed at her, and actively placed the brick and concrete blocks on the grassy ground.

"I am telling you to stop!" Sylph angrily yelled at them.

"You! Stop! Shut your mouth!" One of the unknown men threateningly shouted at her.

Sylph apparently maintained a brave face and instantly responded with extreme anger.

"Stop! It's you all who must stop!"

The unknown men suddenly looked at one another, and two of them roughly held the slender and fair arms of the gentle lady.

One of them threateningly spoke to Sylph. "Lady, it's you who must stop! I'm telling you to leave this place. We will build our corporation here. This vast plain is ours. Nothing belongs to you."

Sylph repeatedly shook her head in disbelief and opposition, and strongly screamed. "No!"

The unknown man swiftly and forcefully slapped her gentle face.

She simply maintained a brave face and assuredly spoke. "You all will regret. What you destroy will destroy you back. I will be the air you breathe, the air you poison, and the same air that has you killed."

The unknown man was about to roughly grab her gentle neck, when she suddenly disappeared as if she shockingly turned into air.

The two unknown men that were holding her slender and fair arms, were instantly frightened by the abrupt disappearance of the gentle lady.

All of a sudden, the unknown men clearly heard a mischievous laughter, and in unison they hesitantly lifted their heads to exactly look in the same direction.

In the invisible air, lightly floating was Sylph whose human figure was slowly disappearing in the air.

Sylph quietly turned her light and disappearing figure around, with a menacing look and smile, and gradually turned invisible.

About the Author

Ancel Mondia

Ancel Mondia is an NBDB-registered Ilongga writer, awarded as Fiction - Woman Writer of the Year 2023 by Ukiyoto Publishing, and a graduate of Master of Arts in English and Literature.

www.ingramcontent.com/pod-product-compliance
Lightning Source LLC
LaVergne TN
LVHW041602070526
838199LV00046B/2093